- **Apatosaurus** was a huge plant eater and could nibble the leaves at the tops of trees.

...s a lizard with a "sail" ...d it lived on land.

- **Allosaurus,** related to Tyrannosaurus, also ate meat and walked on two strong legs.

- **Saltopus** might have been a small early dinosaur. Its bones were found in a sandstone quarry in Scotland.

...s a ferocious ... with teeth that ...ix feet.

IF I MET A DINOSAUR

Written and Illustrated by
Candace Whitman

Derrydale Books
New York • Avenel

Dedicated to

The Children of Daniel Webster Magnet School

Published by Derrydale Books,
distributed by Random House Value Publishing, Inc.,
40 Engelhard Avenue,
Avenel, New Jersey 07001

Designed by Bill Akunevicz Jr.
Production supervised by Roméo Enriquez

Printed and bound in the United States

Library of Congress Cataloging-in-Publication Data

Whitman, Candace, 1958–
If I met a dinosaur / Candace Whitman.
p.   cm.
Summary: Illustrations and rhyming text
present some different kinds of dinosaurs,
including Allosaurus, Dimetrodon, Saltopus, and Pteranodon.
ISBN 0-517-10150-5
[1. Dinosaurs—Fiction.   2. Stories in rhyme.]   I. Title.
PZ8.3.W6114If   1994
[E]—dc20
94-15120
CIP   AC

8 7 6 5 4 3 2 1

If I met Apatosaurus,

The first thing I'd check

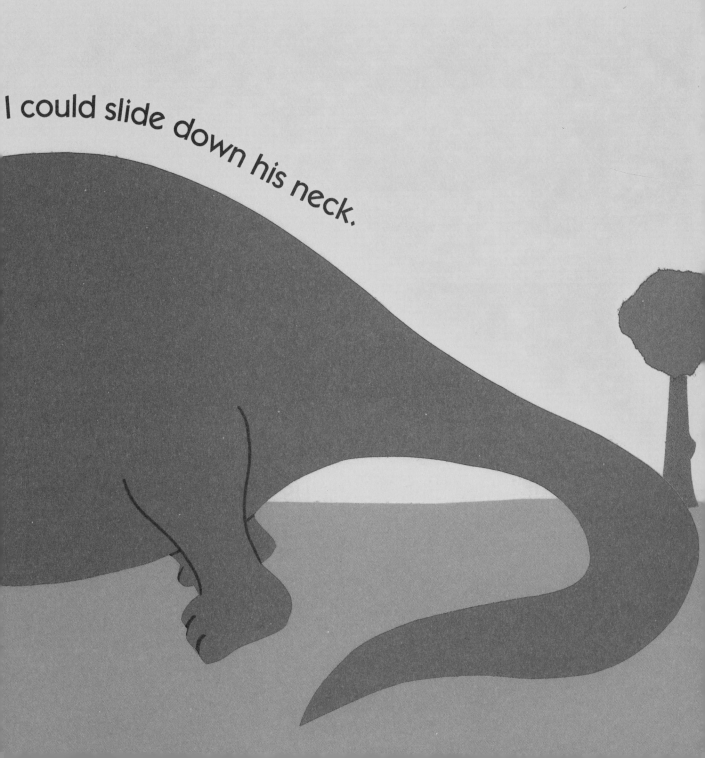

If I met Stegosaurus,
       I'd teach him to fight,

Polish his armor,
And make him a knight.

If I met Allosaurus,
I'd like it a bunch,

Unless by some chance
She hadn't had lunch.

If I met Iguanodon,
    And I started to dance,

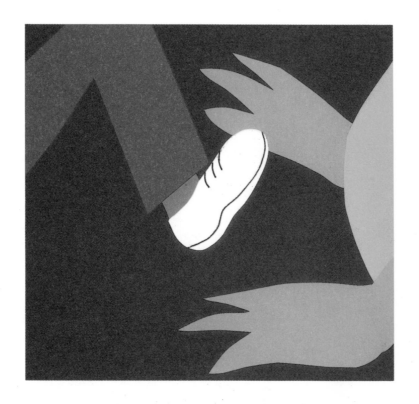

    I'd step on her feet
        To avoid a romance.

If I met Dimetrodon,
And he knew how to float,

With the help of a breeze

He could be a sailboat.

If I met Saltopus,
He'd sit on a shelf,

And season the soup
All by himself.

If I met Tyrannosaurus,
To tell you the truth,

If I met Ichthyosaurus,
    I'd take her to school,

So she'd learn to read

All the signs at the pool.

If I met Pteranodon,

And he liked to glide,

I'd start a new airline—

AIR DINORIDE.

If I met a dinosaur,

It would be so much fun...

DINOSAURS YOU'VE
MET IN THIS BOOK–

Ichthyosaurus lived u
and had a long, poi

Dime
on it'

Tyrannosaur
meat-eating
could be a

Stegosaurus had armor and spikes
which may have been used for protection.

Pteranodon flew the Cretaceous skies
with wings that spread 27 feet!

Iguanodon was one of the first
dinosaurs ever discovered. Its thumb
stuck out like a hitchhiker's!